Ghost

Guido Van Genechten

meadowside
CHILDREN'S BOOKS

If I were a Ghost...

I'd fly round the top of the castle,

and creep up on
all my friends.

I'd dress up to scare!

And win all the spookiest prizes.

I'd draw all the dreamiest Pictures,

then I'd eat all my favourite food.

I'd choose the biggest balloon from my Dad,

I'd have
the best
ghost dreams
ever.

Meadowside Children's Books
185 Fleet Street
London
EC4A 2HS

This edition published 2007
Illustrations © Guido Van Genechten 2006
The right of Guido Van Genechten to be identified
as the illustrator of this work has been asserted by him
in accordance with the Copyright, Designs and Patents Act, 1988

A CIP catalogue record for this book is available
from the British Library
10 9 8 7 6 5 4 3 2
Printed in China